Casey and Callie Cupcake

Sarviol Publishing
Copyright © Nick Rokicki and Joseph Kelley, 2013

ISBN: 978-1479118939

Special wholesale and re-sale rates are available. For more information,
please contact Deb Harvest at petethepopcorn@gmail.com

When purchasing this book, please consider purchasing
an additional copy to donate to your local library.

D1445289

Casey and Callie Cupcake

WRITTEN BY NICK ROKICKI & JOSEPH KELLEY
ILLUSTRATED BY RONALDO FLORENDO

It was a boring day in the shop until Casey and Callie were baked.

This couple of Chocolate Cupcakes were sure to be a catch!

"Oh no, you're not," cackled Callie, sitting near the cupboard.

"Food fight!" "Food fight!" "Food fight!"
The chorus of catcalls was started by
Paula the 'Pretty in Pink' Cupcake and soon
Shelly the 'Snickerdoodle' Cupcake had joined in
...Not to mention Ruthie the Rich Red Velvet Cupcake!

"Calm! Calm,"
came the voice of Crusty the Carrot Cupcake,
the oldest cupcake in the shop. He cast his eyes toward
Casey and Callie and said,
"you're both clever Cocoa Cupcakes!
Now cool your frosting!"

Callie got a crazy look in her eyes as she gazed at cups lined up the counter. They were filled with all sorts of different cupcake toppings!

Quick like a cat, Callie jumped into the first cup! Now Callie the Chocolate Cupcake was completely covered in Chocolate Sprinkles!

Casey caved in to his desire to outdo Callie-- and he crudely jumped into the next cup! Casey emerged dripping in little bits of White Chocolate flakes.

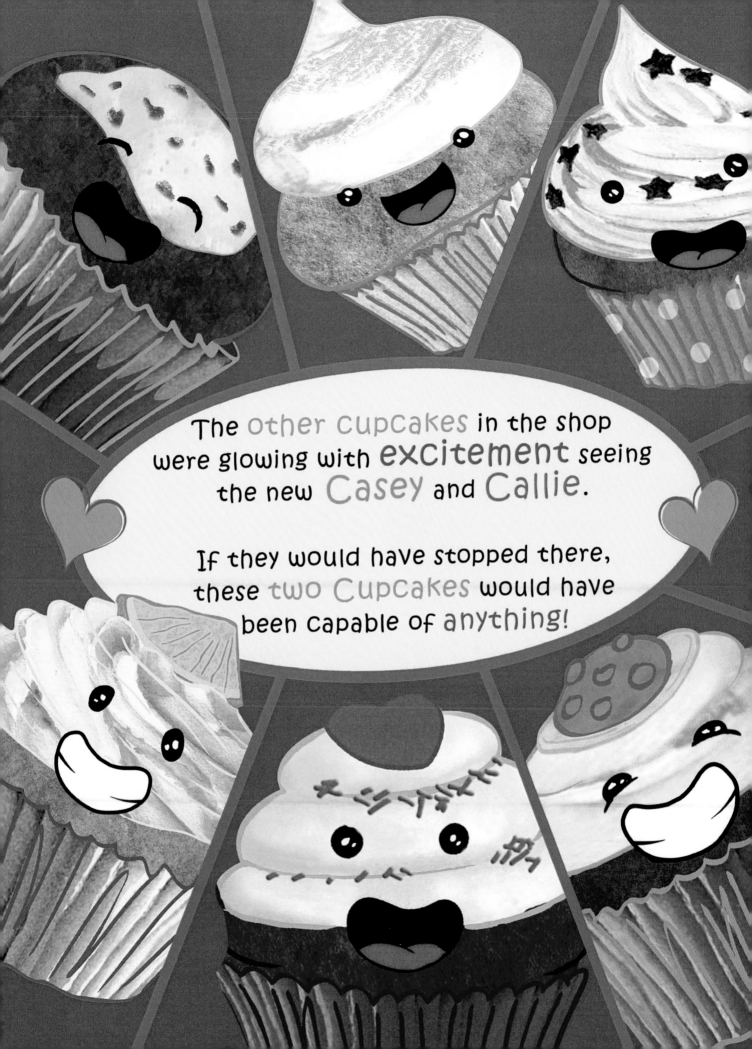

The other cupcakes in the shop were glowing with excitement seeing the new Casey and Callie.

If they would have stopped there, these two cupcakes would have been capable of anything!

 "I'm still better," crowed Callie!

"I don't think so," countered Casey!

Then the cupcakes began jumping,
left and right!

Callie curiously swam in caramel!

Casey clomped into the cream cheese!

Casey
came tumbling
into the Cranberry!

Casey and Callie looked at each other. They were confused! Why were these other cupcakes saying these things?

Surely, the more glitz and glamour and toppings they had, the better and more special they were? Correct?

"Nobody is going to like a
Chocolate Cupcake covered in
Chocolate Sprinkles, Carrots, Caramel,
Coffee and Cheddar Cheese"
said Crusty to Callie.

"And you'll go nowhere with White Chocolate Flakes, Cashews, Cream Cheese, Cranberries and Curry," Crusty explained to Casey.

Casey and Callie crossed the counter to the mirror. Crusty was right-- they were ruined! Nobody would take them home, now.

Callie and Casey eyed the cups... Together, they both jumped at the same time -- into butterscotch frosting!

When they were done with that, they waded into the vanilla sprinkles... Callie and Casey wanted to be a cute couple!

Just then, a lady wearing
a uniform walked into the shop.
She said, "may I please have two
Chocolate Cupcakes with the flavor
of butterscotch and vanilla?
And maybe a raspberry on top?"

Two raspberries capped
the cupcakes!

For the record, Lori Jacobs and Dana Iliev are just as pretty in person as their illustrations in Casey and Callie Cupcake… and their cupcakes taste just as amazing as they look in Ronaldo Florendo's depiction.

Cake in a Cup!

Natives of Toledo, Ohio, Lori and Dana opened Cake in a Cup in their hometown in 2008, starting their business and their cupcakes from scratch. The pair use 100% real ingredients like vanilla and cream cheese in the frosting, along with local lemons and fresh blueberries where the recipes call.

In 2011, Food Network's Cupcake Wars contacted Lori and Dana to take part in the reality television baking competition. Surprising nobody but themselves, they won 1st place with a chocolate batter cupcake prepared with stout beer, frosted with dark chocolate ganache. The movie-themed cupcake was topped with a puff of lime green buttercream, studded with chocolate chips, making it look like a mushroom!

Learning through this experience that creativity pays, Lori and Dana decided to team up with authors Joe Kelley and Nick Rokicki to promote literacy and learning in local schools, through Casey and Callie Cupcake.

With this partnership, we hope to teach kids that reading is of the utmost importance and also engage parents in the educational process. Cupcakes and learning… what a great combination! To learn more about Cake in a Cup, visit www.CakeInACup.com or come see Lori and Dana at their store: 6801 W. Central Ave., Toledo, Ohio 43617.

Ronaldo Florendo!

http://www.behance.net/rmflorendo14

Ronald, as he would like to be simply called, is a year 2000 Architecture graduate in Manila.

Fast forward 2008, only as a part-time gig, he was commissioned to do his very first Children's Book. Surprisingly, demand for his work started pouring and the rest as they say is history.

Presently, he's doing book illustrations as a full-time job, and when he's on a break you can usually catch him chilling on white sand.

A Note From Nick and Joe...

We are both completely humbled by the outpouring of support for our books and projects over the past year. Casey and Callie Cupcake was a true labor of love, fueled by our belief that the story is awesome and the message is needed. Children today are just too wrapped up in material things— they are too quick to look past someone's heart and personality to pass judgements.

There are certain people that must be thanked for their help in launching this title:

Collin and Gavin Wendt, keep on reading! Knowledge is power! You're lucky to have the Mommy and Daddy that you do...

Lori Opp, co-author Joe Kelley has known you since junior high school and always remembers you for your loyalty and friendship. As an adult, you've retained those qualities and even strengthened them. Thank you.

The Simons Family: Chad, Kim, Chad Jr., Keira and Camdyn, what great parents you have, that take an active interest in your education— always value that!

Emilia and Jaidyn Fernandez, who we met in Lexington, Kentucky on our Encouragement Across America Tour, you were so excited to have your Pete the Popcorn book signed! But we were even more excited to meet you!

Patterson Elementary School in Tecumseh, Michigan was one of the most special schools we visited through our travels. Michele Sanders, who organized the visit, should be commended for her commitment to the education of children.

Warrenwood Elementary School in Fayetteville, North Carolina was another standout. Jennifer Archer is an awesome and dedicated teacher that we met in a Detroit suburb. After moving to North Carolina, she kept us in mind and invited us to her new school. There, we were able to meet students Allyson Linn, Jordan Brown and Crystal Mumford. These kids were great and we'd like to remind them to always encourage each other!

Callie House was a parent that we met in North Carolina. When she found out that our next project was titled Casey and Callie Cupcake, she approached us after our presentation to tell us her story. Thanks for sharing, Callie.

Tegan Schott, always take pride in your family and follow the footsteps of your Mom.

To the best pilot in the world, Kevin Rush: don't chew gum and sell wine at the same time.

Calla, Trevor, Nathaniel and Abigail Teague, reading every
day is the best way to become a great learner and keep your childlike creativity.

Gabby Riley at Sts. Peter and Paul School in Cary, Illinois. You're a great student!!!

Callie Moore, your name is in the book! Make sure you always ask your
Mom for help with homework— she was the smartest one in the classroom!

Shawn Reber, Kitty Cat Manor is our favorite place to recharge and brainstorm ideas!

To both of our Moms, Sandra Jean and Sondra Jean, we talk a lot about encouragement.
Nowhere in our lives did we find more encouragement than from you.

Finally, everyone always asks, "how do you guys come up with this stuff?"

The answer is quite simple: personal experiences, family, friends.
In this case, a family recipe from Carolyn Goetz. At every family function,
Carolyn bakes up these cupcakes, one of Nick's favorites. Here is the recipe... and
if you make them, post a picture on Facebook at www.Facebook.com/CupcakeBook

From the Kitchen of Carolyn Goetz

Black Bottom Cupcakes

1 - 8 oz. Package Cream Cheese, softened 1 - Egg 1/3 Cup White Sugar
Beat these together until smooth, then stir in 1 - 12 ounce package of chocolate
chips before setting aside. Then, mix one box of chocolate cake mix according
to package directions. Fill cupcake papers 1/3 full of cake batter. Then, place
one teaspoon of cream cheese mixture on top. Bake at 350 degrees for
18-20 minutes. You can top with chopped nuts or colored sugar...
but to eat them like Carolyn's, leave them plain--- no frosting!
This is the way Nick's family have been enjoying them for years!

Made in the USA
San Bernardino, CA
12 December 2014